How Come You're So Shy?

By Leone Castell Anderson
Illustrated by J. Ellen Dolce

A GOLDEN BOOK • NEW YORK

Western Publishing Company, Inc., Racine, Wisconsin 53404

A B C D E F G H I J

It was early morning. Ashley was playing on her swing set. She pumped her legs to make the swing go. She went higher and higher. And she sang.

Ashley loved to swing and sing, especially when she was alone and no one could hear her.

Suddenly Ashley stopped singing. She heard
voices coming from the yard next door. There
were her new neighbors, who had just moved in.

"Hello," Mrs. Raleigh called to her.
"Would you like to come over and play with
Melinda?"

Ashley ducked her head and pretended not to
hear.

"Don't be shy," she heard Mrs. Raleigh say.

Ashley sighed. Everyone always said that to her. She looked over at Melinda and her mother. "I have to get ready for school," Ashley said.

Just then, Ashley's mother called to her. Ashley jumped off the swing and went inside the house.

"Ashley," said her mother, "please go to the bakery and get a loaf of bread for breakfast. But hurry. You don't want to be late for school."

Ashley ran down the block to the bakery. She waited in line. Just as it was her turn, a man came into the store and stepped up to the counter in front of her.

Mr. Erickson, the baker, looked at Ashley. "Isn't it your turn?" he asked.

"Yes," she said softly.

"Well, don't be so shy, Ashley," said Mr. Erickson.

Ashley nodded. She bought a loaf of bread and took it home.

After breakfast, Ashley put on her jacket and picked up her books.

"Why don't you ask Melinda to walk to school with you?" asked her mother.

"But, Mom, I don't know her yet."

"That would be a good way to get to know her." Ashley's mother gave her a smile and a hug.

Outside, Ashley saw Melinda coming out of her house. Ashley paused. She thought it might be nice to walk to school with Melinda.

"Hi, Melinda," she said, but her words didn't come out very loudly.

Melinda looked away, as if she hadn't heard Ashley.

Sara, a girl from Ashley's class, came running down the sidewalk.

"Come on, Ashley," she yelled. "I'll race you to the corner."

"Okay," said Ashley. She looked back at Melinda and thought, "Maybe she doesn't want to walk with me, anyhow."

At school, Ashley watched Mr. Morrell print letters on the board. Ashley wriggled with excitement. She thought she knew what they spelled.

Mr. Morrell asked the class, "Who can tell me what words I've written here?"

Autumn
pumpkin
Indian corn
haystack
acorn
frost

7:00 am
7:30 am
8:00 am

"I know, I know," Sara called out, waving both hands.

Ashley wanted to raise her hand, too. But she was afraid of being wrong.

Mr. Morrell turned to Melinda. "Maybe our new girl knows," he said. "Can you tell us the words, Melinda?"

Melinda's face turned pink. "I—I—" she stuttered.

Ashley wondered if Melinda was afraid of being wrong, too.

"She's just shy, Mr. Morrell," Sara said loudly.

"That's all right, Melinda," said Mr. Morrell. Then he called on Sara.

"I DID know the words," Ashley told herself as she listened to Sara read them off the board.

Autumn
pumpkin
Indian corn
hayrack
acorn
frost

7:00 am
7:30 am
8:00 am

At recess, Ashley saw Melinda standing alone. "I could ask her if she'd like to swing," Ashley thought.

Suddenly Sara called out, "Why don't you talk, Melinda?"

Melinda ducked her head.

Ashley knew why. "I pretend not to hear people, too," she thought. "Especially when I don't know what to say. Maybe Melinda and I are alike."

"You don't have to answer Sara," Ashley said to Melinda.

Sara walked up to Melinda and asked, "How come you're so shy?"

"Oh, Sara!" Ashley scolded.

At that moment, Mr. Morrell called to everyone.
"We're going to play kick-ball today. Ashley, you'll
be one of the captains. Choose your team."
Sara and the other children danced around
Ashley, shouting, "Pick me! Pick me!"

Ashley saw Melinda standing quietly behind the
others. She knew how Melinda felt.
   Suddenly Ashley knew what she wanted to do.

"Make up your mind, Ashley," said Mr. Morrell. "Who's your first choice?"

Ashley took a deep breath. "I choose Melinda," she said.

She saw a smile spread across Melinda's face. Ashley smiled, too.

When school was out, Sara nudged Ashley and yelled, "I'll race you home!"

"No, thanks," Ashley said. "I want to walk home with Melinda." Ashley turned to Melinda and said, "Okay?"

Melinda looked pleased. "Okay," she said.

As they walked along together Ashley said, "I think my favorite thing to do is swing."

"Mine, too," Melinda said softly. "I love to swing."

"You do?" Ashley began to skip. "Then let's go swing on my swings."

The two girls laughed as they ran to Ashley's backyard.

The girls pumped their legs to make the swings go. As they went higher and higher Ashley heard someone singing. It was Melinda.

Ashley gave a happy sigh. And she began to sing, too.